The Givenchy Code

Ptolemy Pecksniff
And Ron Nolan

Forward by Guy Noir

Dorkshire House
London * New York

DEDICATION

To fellow Chucklebumms,
whomever and wherever
they might be.

"Those who were seen dancing were thought to be insane by those who could not hear the music."

- Friedrich Nietzsche

FORWARD

By Guy Noir

Who the devil is Ptolemy Pecksniff? Imagine my chagrin when invited to pen an introduction to a noir crime novel by an unknown author whom I had never heard of—precisely, I suppose, because he was so utterly unknown.

However, I do seem to remember some years ago sharing an elevator with an absurdly nondescript fellow vaguely resembling the author. As I recollect, it was shortly before they razed the old, crumbling Acme building where I used to sit many dark nights in my twelfth floor office in a city that knew how to keep its secrets, contemplating the answers to life's persistent questions.

Imagine my surprise to find that Pecksniff, a fellow private eye, hails from Dorkshire, England, where he achieved international fame by solving the sensational Chucklebumm murder case. His exploits have been subsequently heralded in the bestselling novel, *Murder Most Heinous*, by Chesney Chucklebumm.

Be that as it may, as children we are taught that if we do not have something good to say, to say nothing at all. It behoves me, then, to remain silent concerning the dubious value of Ptolemy Pecksniff's literary pretentions.

Nevertheless, I do side with Albert Einstein, in that, "Reality is merely an illusion, albeit a very persistent one."

CHAPTER 1

Izzy Einstein, the ill-acclaimed and somewhat addled second cousin to the great physicist, Albert Einstein, found himself in deep cah-cah with feminists when he remarked, "Um Himmels Willen! Gesundheit, Ich fresse einen Besen, und so weiter..." This cryptic and wholly imparsable German phrase, when unzipped, translates loosely to English as, "For heaven's sake! In the universal scheme of things, women are simply nature's way of making more men," or something to that effect.

Philosopher Friedrich Nietzsche, an equally rabid chauvinist, proclaimed, "Ah, women. They make the highs higher and the lows more frequent," as well as, "The true man wants two things: danger and play. For that reason he wants woman, as the most dangerous plaything." We gratuitously note that this is the same Friedrich who lamented, "In heaven, all of the interesting people are missing."

In a similar vein, the preeminent philosopher Emmanuel Kant, mentally exhausted upon completion of his monumental work *A Critique of Pure Reason* was heard to muse, "Gunter glieben glauben globen!"

As we can see then, at least two of the world's greatest minds are in accord when it comes to the crucial and indeed central role of the *femme fatale* (along with her younger version, the *fille fatale*) in the noir detective genre.

Einstein and Nietzsche could not help but notice that it is invariably the hot vampy dame, accompanied by the siren song of moaning saxophones, who arrives to kick off the story action and subsequently seduce our hero into an asymmetrical relationship. Driving him to the point of obsession and exhaustion, she thereby renders him incapable of making rational decisions—a warning to us all to avoid asymmetrical relationships.

As Izzy was fond of saying, "Achtung, fertig, los!" So with the above firmly in mind, let us now turn to a subject most near and dear to my heart, namely me—the quintessential private eye *me*, that is. In order to gain a proper perspective of my profession, we must first understand that private eyes are many things to many people: private investigator (PI), dick, private dick, gumshoe, shamus, sleuth, slewfoot, snoop, peeper, busybody, butt-in, ferret, meddler, peeping Tom, rubberneck, quidnunc, scumbag, dog breath, fink, SOB, and, not least, pragmatic existentialist. The list could go on of course, but why needlessly offend the squeamish?

I would caution career-seekers that the life of a private eye is not for everyone. One must have the appetite for an occasional knuckle sandwich and possess a sufficiently resilient skull to absorb repeated hammering by very hard objects, namely gun butts and tire irons. It goes without saying that one ought be tough as nails, thick-skinned, hard-boiled, hard drinking, have a cast-iron stomach and a well-oiled, inflatable libido.

Do not be fooled by Hollywood's version of the P.I. One's days and nights are not necessarily spent on the razor's edge of imminent danger, cruising society's gritty underbelly tracking down thuggish malefactors and hanging out in slimy booze joints. Rather, one must be ready to cope with days, even weeks, of unmitigated tedium punctuated by moments of utter boredom.

My profession does have its unique compensations, chief among them the libidinous, drop-dead gorgeous babes parading in and out of one's office and generally getting underfoot. Although I have yet to fathom precisely why we private dicks have such a profound aphrodisiacal effect on women, I do suspect it has something to with our impeccable diction and guileless, unprepossessing demeanor.

To graphically illustrate the aforementioned, I offer the following true story, based on a fictional account selected at random from my files—a task made simple due to the fact that it has been my long-standing practice to file my cases in random order should just such a contingency arise.

If at times readers find the following story somewhat bizarre or disconcertingly obtuse, they may take comfort in Nietzsche's keen observation, "Those who were seen dancing were thought to be insane by those who could not hear the music."

I do so hope you enjoy the music.

And trust me: one simply cannot make this stuff up.

CHAPTER 2

Why not begin our story at the beginning? I was loitering as usual in what I risibly refer to as my office on the tenth floor of the decrepit soon-to-be-demolished Acme Building. Of all the crummy office buildings in all the world, did they really have to choose mine for imminent implosion? Mid-morning tomorrow, the place would be a pile of smoldering rubble. Actually, I might not have minded so much had we not recently shampooed the carpets.

It was of course hellishly difficult to concentrate amid the chattering din of jackhammers, to say nothing of the parade of large men in hardhats clomping about planting sticks of dynamite floors below.

In the interest of full disclosure, I must confess that I suffer from chronic "Generalized Asininity Avoidance Syndrome," or (GAAS). This rare neurological disorder prevents one from abiding fools, morons, and their cretinous cousins, imbeciles. In the company of such I tend to become unhinged. Not only might I fly off the handle at the slightest provocation, but in extreme circumstances am prone to break out in hives.

With all the devilish racket and hubbub whirling about, I felt a desperate need to decompress. Sinking into my squeaking swivel chair, I plopped my size twelve's on the desk, closed my eyes, and dropped into a deep, meditative trance—known to the unenlightened as a snooze.

My impish karmic destiny, however, had other plans. My blissful interlude was shattered by the imperious buzzing of the intercom. *An intercom with an attitude!* Precisely what I did not need at the moment, for I had of late developed a contentious relationship with all things mechanical. An imperious machine was quite enough to send me over the edge.

Fortunately, my yoga training kicked in. I smoothly swung my feet from the desk, sprang forward and punched the receiver button, all in one fluid, graceful motion. "Yes..?"

"A call for you on line two, boss."

"Who is it?"

"It's me, your secretary, boss. You know, Susie…"

My jaw muscles worked involuntarily. My right eye began twitching spasmodically. My GAAS symptoms seemed to be growing more severe by the day. I had recently acquired a repertoire of nervous tics, and certain parts of my body had begun taking on a life of their own.

"Yes, yes, I know who *you* are, Susie secretary," I fumed. "But who is it on the phone?"

"You mean besides me, boss?"

"Yes, Susie, the person who called in…"

"A female sir."

"A female sir? What the blazes is a female sir? Half man, half woman—a hermaphrodite?"

"No, boss, a woman…"

"Great! Now that we have the caller's gender down pat, I presume this woman has a name?"

"Everybody's got a name, don't they, boss?"

"Quite right, Susie—well, what is it then?"

"What is what, boss?"

"Her name, the woman's name, Susie!" My left eyebrow began to flutter, joining the chorus of facial spasms. "The woman's name!" I cajoled. "For God's sake, Susie, what is the woman's name?"

"It's one of those weird foreign names, boss. I really can't pronounce—"

"Oh, never mind…!"

Wrestling down a demonic fit of pique, I snatched up the phone receiver. "Rentadick Investigations…"

CHAPGER 3

The dame's sultry voice sizzling the wire was a warm questing tongue wantonly caressing one's ear: "*Oh, please*, Mr. Rentadick! I implore you…I vaunt you to help me. You must...I—"

Vavoom! The receiver grew hot in my sweaty palm…hotter; I envisioned phone lines melting.

Then it struck me: She had erringly pronounced "want" as "vaunt," a linguistic anomaly ripe for analysis. First off, the throaty, silken tenor of her voice ruled out any guttural Teutonic influence. Her sibilant diphthongs and syllabic consonants suggested Polish or perhaps Basque…and yet…. Definitely Slavic, I concluded, with a distinct hint of Mongol. My best guess was that her ancestral digs lie between the The Volga and Oka rivers, somewhere west of the Ural Mountains….

"Mr. Rentadick! *Please!* You are there, Mr. Rentadick?"

"Wha…ah, yes, present and accounted for," I exclaimed, roused from my dialectal musings.

"Mr. Rentadick, *please*—"

"I am really very sorry," I said, "but there is no Mr. Rentadick."

"Vhat? You are saying there is *no* Mr. Rentadick?"

"Yes… No, I mean, no—on second thought, I do mean yes." I said. "Look, I'll be brutally explicit…Mr. Rentadick does not exist."

"Oy! Why is this? Did poor man die? Do I send flowers?"

"You can forget the flowers—and, no, he did not die," I explained. "You see, he never was, never has been, and most likely never will be."

The dame's tremulous, exotic voice displayed a frisson of panic, "Oy, oy, in my terror-stricken frame of mind I have dialed the wrong—"

"No, no, you have the right number," I hastily cut in, lest she prematurely interrupt our verbal intercourse. "But you see, Rentadick is the name of a company, not the name of an actual living person."

"But companies are people, too, are they not?"

"The U.S. Supreme Court does seem to think so," I conceded her point. "However, one cannot thereby assume there be a Mr. Acme or a Mr. Home Depot, a Mr. Kinkos, a Mr.—"

"Ya, but if you are not Mr. Rentadick, to whom am I speakink?"

Speakink? Again, a minor linguistic incongruity served to confirm my previous analysis. I was reminded once again that being an English major with a minor in Library Science does occasionally pay off. As a matter of fact, I suddenly flashed back on how I had solved a most heinous murder case some years ago when….

The dame's plaintive wail begged my attention, "Please, whoever strange person you are—to whom am I speakink?"

"You are speakink—or rather *speaking*—," I said, "to Ptolemy Pecksniff, P.I. At your service, Madame."

"Is okay I ask if P is really necessary?"

I sat for a moment in stunned silence before answering, "Is the P really necessary, you ask? Silly woman! Of course the P is necessary," I explained with a whiff of indignation. "Without the P, Pecksniff comes off Ecksniff, which is not my name. I grant you that it could easily be someone else's name but it is definitely not *my* name."

"Nyet—I am to mean *Ptolemy*. Is there not a silent P in Ptolemy?"

"A silent P in Ptolemy?" However does one come up with such a ridiculous notion? I wondered. "Why should one consider there to be a silent P?" I asked, incredulous.

"So that one maybe does not have to pronounce the P?"

I watched fascinated as the fingers of my left hand, of themselves, began drumming the desk in an erratic tattoo—rat-a-tat-tat, tippy-tippy-tap…

"Then why have a P at all?" I countered. "It makes no sense to have a P there, if you're not going to pronounce it, now does it? Besides, my dear mother insisted that I always pronounce my Ps."

"Could you not have heard dear mother wrong?" the dame purred. "Maybe she did mean for you to eat your peas like good little boy."

I thoughtfully stroked my noble chin. "Um…a distinct possibility, I grant you that," I conceded. "Yes, peas *were* yet another of mother's pet issues. Ptolemy, she would often say—"

"There again you go!"

"There again I go, what?" I inquired.

"You are saying out loud the silent P!"

"As one must do," I asserted, "if they wish to be precise about it, for God's sake!"

I observed with some consternation that my fist was pounding the desk of its own accord.

"But it is difficult," the dame complained, "to get one's tongue and lips into proper way to say…"

I paused and took a deep yogic breath to regain control of my racing pulse. How utterly maddening that I must continually coach people how to correctly pronounce my name! Yet this squirrely dame would not destroy my equanimity. Lapsing into emergency mode, I began my sonorous yoga breathing exercise.

"Vhat is funny noise that you now make?" the dame wanted to know.

"It's called breathing," I said.

"Vhat you are, pervert? You always breathe heavy on phone when talk to woman?"

"Watch whom call you a pervert," I protested. "I'll have you know it's a free country, I can breathe however I want."

"Ya, but why do you breathe at me in such a naughty way?"

"Look," I said, "I am not breathing *at* you, lady! I am just—oh, forget it. Can we please return to the matter at hand?"

"And vhat is matter you have in hand?" she cooed. "Is bigger than bread box?"

"I'll have you know there is nothing in my hands except the telephone receiver."

"Ya, is likely story…" she crooned silkily. "Maybe you vaunt now to talk some dirty to me? You vaunt—"

"No! I don't *want* anything of the kind!"

"Oy, but maybe I like you to talk some dirty. You vaunt to know vhat I am not wearink? You will have big surprise…"

"Look," I said, "I haven't time for such indecorous nonsense. Can we get on with how to properly pronounce my name? Let's proceed phonetically, shall we? Can you say "Ptui?"

"Ya, I do think so…*Ptui*…"

"Again," I demanded. "Only this time with more emphasis on the P…*P-tui!*"

"*P-tui*…"

"Good girl. And now can you say *P*-tolemy?"

"*P-tuilemy.*"

I heaved a sigh, resigning myself once again to ignominious defeat. "Damn it all—just call me Tolly, would you!"

"*P-tolly?*"

"No! No, and no again…" I corrected vehemently. "There's no P in Tolly!"

"So it is Tolly, then…without P?"

"There you have it!"

Bathed in perspiration, pulse pounding, I fell back into my chair, kicked off my shoes, jerked my tie loose and tore open my shirt collar. I needed a breather, time out, a moment to relax and recoup my *savoir faire.*

But it was not to be.

CHAPTER 4

The dame was shrieking, "Mr. Pecksniff! You are there, Mr. Pecksniff? Why do you not speak?"

"Yes, yes, yes," I responded wearily. "I am totally here and now, attentive to the eternal moment."

"Vhat?"

"Look," I said, "would you please tell me how I might be of service, Miss...I'm sorry, I didn't catch your name."

"Pantzaroff..."

I came upright in my chair. "Excuse me, would you mind repeating—?"

"I am Polinovska Pantzaroff," she elaborated. "My father, he was Russian."

"Did I ask your father's nationality?" I responded irascibly. "So what if your father *was* Russian? That's nothing, *my* mother was Egyptian." Her cavalier manner had set me off. There is nothing worse in my book than a dame with snippy attitude; as it was, my nerves were now taut as over-tuned guitar strings and might begin pinging at any moment.

She interjected hurtfully, "Ya, and that is how you get dumb name, *P-tuilemy?*"

I took unbridled umbrage at her tone of voice. "Don't get snooty with me," I said. "I'll have you know my ancestors were the little brown people who built the pyramids."

"And I vaunt to know vhat has that to do with price of tea in China?"

"Since you've raised the subject," I rejoined, "*my* father was Chinese—so there!"

"*Nyah, Nyah!* You think I am interested in your genital history, Mr.—vhat is name again, Peckerhead?"

"*Pecksniff!*" I reminded her none too gently. "Now look here, if you don't mind, I think it best you call me Tolly. And might I call you Polly? You know, Polinovska...Polly...?"

"Nyet! I do not vaunt yet to be on inanimate first name basis with man with such dumb name as *P-tuilemy.*"

"I assume you mean to say 'intimate'," I corrected.

"Vhat! Now you are to tell me vhat to say?" the dame bristled. "You do not tell me vhat it is I mean!"

"Fine, fine, fine," I said, stifling a frisson of ire as my left leg commenced dancing. "Have it your way, if you must. It's no skin off the nether region of my anatomy. Henceforth I shall refer to you by your ridiculously droll surname. Now again, what might I do for you, Miss Pantzaroff?"

"Wait, wait!" she said. "Vhat is funny noise I hear—sound like crick...crick?"

"I happen to be cracking my knuckles," I informed. "Do you mind?"

Why was it that my clients these days, especially those of the female gender, were so invariably argumentative? I was beginning to understand why my great noir detective heroes slapped their women around. Except for Charlie Chan, that is. Charlie was a real gent; you never saw ol' Charlie slapping dames around…at least not in public.

"Vhat you can do for me," said Miss Pantzaroff, "is that I have big problem and hope Mr. Rentadick can help me. But you say there is no Mr. Rentadick alive in person. So maybe you will take case, ya?"

Now was the time to roll out my famous Bogart imitation. I stretched my lips over my teeth and said with a sexy, snarling lisp, "Well, that all depends, doll. Upon a variety of factors and things, see. Here's lookin' at you, kid, and what exactly is the nature of your problem, sister?"

"Nyet! I am not sister!" the dame yowled. "And why do you now talk again funny?"

"You think Bogart is funny?"

"I think is stupid! I do not listen to stupid—"

"Okay, okay," I said. "For Pete's sake, I'm sorry! Of course you're not my sister. I was just doing Bogart, is all, and anyway it's just a figure of speech."

"And vhat is figure of speech?"

"My calling you sister…"

"Nyet! I am not sister!"

"All right! All right!" I smacked my forehead. "Good grief, lady, you don't have to bite my head off!"

CHAPTER 5

To control my seething emotions, I pinched my nose between thumb and forefinger and began my yoga alternate nostril breathing exercise, inhaling slowly and calmly in one nostril and exhaling out the other, then reversing the process. At length I leaned back, took a deep breath, and concentrated on slowing my heartbeat.

Next thing I knew, Miss Pantzaroff was shrieking demandingly into the phone, "Mr. Pecksniff! You are there? Why do you not speak? Have you left building and maybe gone to lunch so early, Mr. Pecksniff?"

"Yes, Yes!" I shouted back at her. "I mean 'no' I have not left for lunch! Now might we get this conversation back on track?" I paused to muster what pleasant tone of voice I could under such trying circumstances. "I believe you have a problem you wish to discuss—"

"Before I tell problem," she interrupted imperiously, "I vaunt to know how much you are to charge for case."

I ground my teeth and craned my neck to release the mounting tension....

"Vhat again is funny noise?" the dame wanted to know.

"I was cricking my neck, okay!" I said.

"Cracking knuckles, cricking neck—you are some strange man, I think."

"Look," I sighed, "our standard fee, if you must know, is one hundred dollars a day, plus expenses."

"And how much is expenses?"

I brusquely ticked off a list of the usual expense items. "Well, let's see, there's laundry, pet food and the car needs a tune-up...throw in bullets, whisky, bandages, doctor bills, haircuts and shoe shines, and other such miscellanies and it comes to—"

"Nyet! No, no, I do not vaunt pay for pet food!"

"All right, already!—so no pet food," I said. "We'll scratch the pet food, okay?"

"So how much is without pet food?"

I made a quick mental calculation. "I think we can round it off at a C-note," I said.

"And vhat is C-note of which you speak?"

"Precisely one hundred dollars, unless of course you're paying in rubles."

"Vhat! You are to charge one hundred American dollars a day for expenses? You are capitalist pig!"

"All right. Okay, simmer down, lady..." My teeth were on edge, my nerves frazzled, yet I swallowed my frustration, changed gears and struck a conciliatory note. "Since the customer is king—or *queen* in your case—we are more than willing to compromise. So let's say we drop the itemized expenses and settle for two hundred clams a day."

"And clams is?"

"One clam is approximately one dollar, adjusted for inflation," I explained.

"Two hundred clam dollars for day! You are crooked thief! I will call Better Business Bureau—"

"No, wait! Just wait!" I broke in. "Because it is you, Miss Pantzaroff, and it being the second Tuesday of the month, I'll factor in our standard once-in-a-lifetime promotional discount, plus our senior discount."

"Vhat you think, I am old person?"

"Of course not, Miss Pantzaroff. But I assume you graduated high school and therefore were a senior and thus qualify for our retroactive senior discount. Now, lastly, we must not forget to add in various local, state and federal taxes, plus our extended lifetime satisfaction guarantee, and—let me see here—it all comes down to a very affordable one hundred and ninety-nine dollars and ninety-nine cents per day. So how are we doing so far, Miss Pantzaroff? Sound reasonable?"

"Ya, is less than two hundred bucks for sure!"

I could sense her wavering on the precipice of commitment, so I dropped the clincher, "We'll even throw in a free car wash!"

She lapsed silent. Suspense hung electric in the air as the seconds drug on, then minutes...

At length, I ventured, "You still there, Miss Pantzaroff?"

"Ya, okay. It is deal."

I succumbed to a soupcon of satisfaction over my shrewd salesmanship. One never knew when one's brief employment as a used car salesman might come in handy.

"Do you take credit card?" Miss Pantzaroff wanted to know.

"Sure," I said. "But only after we run your stats against the national FBI database, which can take up to a week, sometimes a month. Plus we charge a twenty percent courtesy fee."

"Then I vaunt to pay with check."

"If you insist," I agreed. "But by the time the check clears our offshore bank, Miss Pantzaroff, you, or more likely I, could be dead, or worse. Of course, if you're in no big hurry..."

"Ya, I am in big hurry. You will take cash?"

"As a last resort, yes," I said. "In unmarked bills, if you don't mind."

"Vhat you mean, unmarked bills?" she cried. "Why is this, Mr. Peckersniff? And do you also vaunt me to wrap money in paper bag and drop off bridge at midnight?"

I chortled condescendingly, "Please, as consenting adults, might we not indulge in sarcasm?"

"Irony is better, you think?"

"No, but ironic sarcasm may be somewhat appropriate under the circumstances," I said. "But, look here, let's get down to business. May I again inquire as to the particular nature of your problem, Miss Pantzaroff?"

"Well," the dame said, her voice quavering, "there is crazy albino person..."

CHAPTER 6

My knee jerked. I did a double, and then a triple, take. "A crazy albino person?" I said. "You mean like in a Dan Brown thriller?"

"Ya, and with tattoos all over body. He follows me everywhere with meat clever."

"Really? I assume you do mean a meat *cleaver.*"

"Ya, and I am so putrefied with fear…"

"I see," I said. "But don't you think your choice of adjective is ill-considered? You obviously mean to say 'petrified', rather than putrefied. You see, putrefied—"

"Do I ask for English lesson?" Miss Pantzaroff was suddenly half screaming, half sobbing. "I do not vaunt for English lesson! Please! I am in terrible fear for life!"

"Okay, Lady, relax," I said. I realized now that I had a damsel in distress on my hands, that I must take manly charge and allay her fears, lest she succumb to maidenly panic. Once again, fate had whipped me up an omelet of mixed metaphors: I must tiptoe through a manic mental minefield, walk a swaying tightrope over the yawning abyss of the subconscious, and dance lightly on psychic eggshells. "Do you have a clue," I asked calmly, "as to why this criminally insane albino fellow is slinking around, drooling at the mouth, following you with murderous intent of chopping you into little bite-sized pieces with his razor sharp meat cleaver?"

The dame's sultry voice dropped to a mere whisper. "I think maybe he vaunts secret information that will explode world."

"And you supposedly possess such information?" I said. "Whatever is the information about?"

"Is about The Givenchy Code."

"Excuse me..." My scalp tingled. I swallowed. "Did you say, The *Givenchy* Code?"

"Do you vaunt me to spell?"

"No, no, any first grader can spell Givenchy," I said. "But if this is anything like the DaVinci Code—"

"Ya, is like that, except is not about bunch of old museums and churches, weirdo priests and loony Pope. Is about fancy clothes..."

My mind raced. "Um, yes, Givenchy.... I suspect, then, it has something to do with the ancient order of Malthusians, an occult society of garment trade workers sworn to guard their earth shattering secret of the ages."

"Ya, and I have key to unlock secret code."

I choked back my rising apprehension. No need for the client to share my hysterical neurosis. I must allay her fears, rein in her raging panic.

Modulating my voice to a lower register, I spoke slowly and soothingly into the receiver, "Now please, Miss Pantzaroff—*do not panic!* There is absolutely no need for panic. Just get a grip on yourself and, again, *don't panic!*

Even though you are in grave peril, *you simply must not panic.*"

"But if not to panic, vhat am I to do?"

"You need to come to my office as soon as possible," I said, "if not sooner."

"But vhat is to do about albino man with meat cleaver?"

"Is he there now?"

"Ya, he waits outside telephone booth for when I come out."

"Put him on," I said. "Let me to talk to him."

"Vhat? You-you vaunt to talk to crazy albino?"

"Not just any crazy albino," I clarified. "Specifically, the one with the meat cleaver."

She was obviously disoriented, hesitant, and debating the issue in her mind, because for a long moment she did not say anything. Then, "Nyet, I do not like idea," she announced. "I think is better I kick crazy albino where he hurt, then I come."

"Okay. But hurry," I said.

"How do I get to office?"

"We're on the tenth floor of what is left of the Acme building," I quickly explained. "If you find yourself at the *Guy Noir* detective agency on the twelfth floor, you've gone too far. So at the tenth floor stop the elevator, take a left and proceed to the door next to the broom closet. Now hurry—"

"Is left or right?"

"Is what left or right?"

"Is broom closet on left or right?"

"Let's see…it will be on your left, presuming that you have taken a left from the elevator. Otherwise, it would be on your right, behind you, and you would have to needlessly retrace your steps. In the interest of time, therefore, I recommend you take a left off the elevator."

"I have got it, ya…"

"Okay, hurry! *No wait*, don't hang up! First, a word of caution," I continued. "If you find yourself in the broom closet, you've gone too far. In that case, you should exit the broom closet, retrace your steps, and take the door immediately to your right—to your right, that is, if you face back in the direction you have come. And, if it hasn't fallen to the floor, you will find my business card, *Rentadick Investigations, P. P. PI*, jammed into a corner of the frosted window glass."

The dame snorted softly, "You are too cheap to vaunt name painted on office window?"

"If you must know, Miss Pantzaroff," I explained with masterly forbearance, "as a franchise operation we require headquarters' approval for all expense items over five dollars. It was hardly our fault that our request for a door sign was forwarded a week after the owners had filed for bankruptcy."

"Oh, that is so awful sad! I had no way to know…"

"No tears, please," I said bravely. "Now quick—duck the albino chap with his cleaver and scoot on over. And, Miss Pantzaroff…"

"Ya…"

"My best advice until then, Miss Pantzaroff..."

"Ya…"

"Tits up!"

"Vhat is this you mean, tits up?"

"It is simply an admonitory ejaculation," I said, "and in no way rises to the level of an aphorism. If you wish, we can discuss it at greater length when you get here. Now hurry! And, above all, *don't panic!*"

I dropped the receiver and collapsed into my squawking swivel chair. There was nothing, absolutely nothing, I could do now but wait and hope against hope. I could scarce keep from gnawing my fingernails to the quick. I rose and paced the room. My mind raced as a thousand questions rattled around inside my battered skull. Would Miss Pantzaroff successfully evade the crazed albino to reach the safety of my office, or might she end up chopped liver in some dark alley? And who or what was behind the vast Givenchy conspiracy? Would we be able to crack the secret code in time? In time for what? I had no idea. Nevertheless, there must be a ticking clock lurking somewhere in order to heighten suspense and drive the story's narrative engine.

The problem came down to this: I knew what I did not know; that was the easy part. The difficulty was that I did not know what I did not know, and that was scary as hell!

But whatever the outcome, I knew one thing for sure: there was simply no way one could make this stuff up.

CHAPTER 7

The Kafkaesque scenario of a crazed albino with a meat cleaver running amok in the city in hot pursuit of Miss Pantzaroff was enough to give me the heebies, if not the geebies. To soothe my jangled nerves, I reached for my smokeless electronic cigarette. I dialed in a healthy dose of nicotine, pressed the power button, leaned back, took a long, deep drag, and filled my lungs with—*nothing!* Infuriated, I whacked the refractory gizmo repeatedly on the corner of the desk and inhaled once again—*nothing squared!* Drat! I had replaced the batteries only yesterday, how could they have expired so soon? Obviously, they had not designed these contraptions with chain smokers in mind.

What was the world coming to when unrepentant nicotine addicts like myself were reduced to sucking on batteries? Would Boggie have appeared on screen with a battery-driven chromium fag dangling insolently from his lips, his eyes narrowed against a tendril of harmless vapor?

What were noir films without ubiquitous clouds of noxious second-hand cigarette smoke swirling about? And figure this—would one fire up a mechanical cigarette after sex? Only, I suppose, if one had indulged in mechanical sex.

Casablanca, The Maltese Falcon, et al, sans cigarettes? Ha!

The intercom buzzed; less imperiously this time, but still I had a mind to hurl the insolent beast out the window. Nevertheless, I stifled the urge, caved into its dictatorial demand and reluctantly punched a button, "Yes...?"—wrong button. I punched another button, "Yes...?" Wrong button. Drat! I punched yet another button, *"Yes?"*

"Line two for you, boss."

"Who is it?"

"It's Susie, boss."

"Susie? Susie who?" I inquired. "Do you have a last name?"

"Queue, boss. Susie Queue..."

"But that's *your* name!" I said. "You're Susie Queue!"

"Yes, boss..."

"My secretary?"

"Yes, boss."

"Swell...now that that's settled, where were we?"

"A call for you, boss, on line two..."

"Line two?"

"Yes, boss."

"Then who's on line one?"

"Nobody, boss."

"Look," I said, "Somebody has to be on line one! For the system to roll over to line two, line one has to be in use. A simple logical deduction, don't you see?"

"But there isn't nobody, boss."

This was absolutely insane! So insane that for the moment I ignored Susie's egregious use of the double negative.

I must get to the bottom of this! "How many lines do we have, Susie?"

"Two, boss..."

"And does anyone ever call in on line one?"

"Not that I know of, boss."

"Then what is the point of such redundancy," I said, "if line one is never used?"

"Maybe it's for us to call out when somebody is calling in..."

"And why would we want to do that?"

"To order a pizza, boss. Or maybe—"

"Never mind, Susie," I said. "Who is it on the line?"

"Which line, boss?"

"The one with the flashing light—line two, I presume."

"The fence department, boss. A Mr. Oreck."

"Fence department?" I remarked redundantly for sake of clarification. "Which fence department?"

"I'm not really sure, boss. Home Depot, maybe?"

"Didn't you bother to ask?" I said. "Good Lord, it could just as well be Lowes or Sears."

"I did ask, but he didn't say—he just said the fence department."

I did not remember ordering any fencing. What on earth would I do with fencing, living in a high-rise apartment building? "Have you by chance ordered fencing lately, Susie?"

"Not that I know of, boss"

This was surely a unadulterated scam, I decided. And, frankly, nothing makes my blood boil more than an unadulterated scam, especially when perpetrated by a pushy fence peddler. Assuming my macho persona, I squared my shoulders and squinted my eyes, *a la* Clint Eastwood. "Have no fear, Susie," I rasped. "I'll handle this. Just leave it to me."

I pulled my .357 Magnum from the desk drawer, checked that it was loaded and snatched up the receiver, "Look, punk," I growled, "this is decidedly *not* your lucky day. If you think for one minute—"

"Who's the ditzy broad?"

I did not appreciate being interrupted mid-sentence by a fence salesman, no matter how authoritative his stentorian voice.

"Which ditzy broad?" I demanded.

"The airhead who answers your phone."

"Airhead? I'll have you know she's my secretary."

"She got a name?"

"Yeah, Susie ..."

"Susie Q, right?"

"Look here," I said, "if you knew her name, why are you asking me?" I paused meaningfully. "And come to think of it, how *did* you know her name?"

"Call it a wild guess..."

I glanced up at the clock and mentally subtracted two hours to account for the fact that we had not reset it the last round of daylight savings. Ten-fifteen A.M. and some odd seconds. Miss Pantzaroff would be arriving any minute...or not, depending upon mid-town traffic and the maniacal determination of the crazed albino.

"Look, Oreck—if that's really your name," I said, "I haven't time for games. I'm dealing with matters of life and death here. So if you're calling from Sears—"

"What the hell makes you think I'm calling from Sears?"

"Okay. Home Depot..."

"Home Depot?"

"All right, Lowes, then—you're calling from Lowes. So I'm telling you," I said, "there's been some mistake. I haven't ordered any fencing that I know of."

"Knock off the chin music, will you, Rentadick! This is urgent!"

"Oh yeah, how urgent?"

"Highest classified national priority, Teflon Three!"

Teflon Three? I was seized by a bout of laughter. "Are you serious? You're trying to sell me Teflon fencing? Who do you think you're talking to, some rube who just fell off the hay wagon? Level with me, Oreck, exactly where *are* you calling from?"

"Defense Department."

"Which fence department?"

"The U.S. Defense Department!"

"U.S. *Defense* Department? Oh…oh, yes, *that* Defense Department…"

"Yeah, *that* Defense Department, dimwit! How many defense departments you think we got?"

"Okay, look," I said, "I really had to file an extension this year. You see, I needed more time…my accountant's mother-in-law's yippy little dog ate my—"

"Christ! We don't give a damn about your taxes, Rentadick! That's for the IRS to worry about. Our job is to run the country's wars and stuff, chase terrorists all over hell and gone, that sort of thing."

"So why are you calling me then?" I said.

"Is this phone secure, Rentadick?"

"Well, it's plugged into the wall, if that's what you mean."

"Good. What we are about to discuss is on a need to know basis, you understand."

"But what if I don't want to know?" I said. "Maybe I would rather not know what I don't know than know what I don't know—and by the way, the name is Pecksniff, Ptolemy Pecksniff!"

"*The* Ptolemy Pecksniff?"

"Yes, *the* Ptolemy Pecksniff." I responded smugly. "You've heard of me then?"

"No, can't say that I have. Some weird name you got though, fella."

"My mother was Egyptian."

"Who cares!"

"I care," I said. "I care very much!"

"Pecksniff, huh? Don't sound very Egyptian to me..."

CHAPTER 8

My eyelids were twitching again, a sure sign that I was fast reaching the frayed end of my tether. What's more, I had neither the time nor the inclination to become involved in this name-game business so soon after my grueling session with Miss Pantzaroff.

Exasperated beyond measure, I exploded out of my swivel chair and onto my feet. "Look!" I said, "I have better things to do this moment than discuss my matrilineal heritage. Now I really must go, I have an important—"

"Sit down, Rentadick!"

The harsh, thunderous voice was that of Lee Marvin portraying a dyspeptic Marine drill sergeant.

"What?" I wanted to know.

"I said, sit down—you're not going anywhere, maggot!"

I froze.

Something very strange and utterly mysterious was going on here. So what *was* going on here? It was time for a little deductive analysis: How could this Oreck fellow, whoever he was, have possibly known that in my exasperation I had exploded from my swivel chair and onto my feet? Employing Occam's Razor, the most obvious answer was that Oreck was psychic, a telepath who could see though walls and such. If one thought out of the box, however, an alternative hypothesis was that the office might be under some sort of video surveillance. Hidden cameras? I glanced quickly at the ceiling, behind the bookcase, under the desk. Nothing that I could see...

I resorted to a brilliant ad hoc strategy, lifting my right foot from the floor.

"Out of curiosity," I asked cagily, "what am I doing just now, Oreck?"

"You are standing on one leg."

"Which one?"

"The left one."

"And now…?"

"The right one."

"And what about now?"

"You're standing on your head," he said. "You want me to tell you which one?"

"Remarkably good guesses," I said. "So again, out of curiosity, where exactly are you are calling from?"

"A stakeout."

"Where?"

"Outback."

"Outback stakeout? You've got to be kid—"

At that, the door to the fire escape burst open and three burly men in suits and buzz cuts flew into the room brandishing pistols and flashing badges. "Freeze, Rentadick! Federal agents! "

CHAPTER 9

I froze.

"Spread 'em, maggot!" They roughly whirled me round, spread-eagled me against my desk and all-too-vigorously patted me down.

"You guys from the TSA?" I mugged.

"Shut up, maggot!"

I shut up.

"Ah-ha, and what do we have here, Rentadick?" The larger of the three suits curiously examined a gleaming cylindrical object.

"Oh that?" I said. "That's my smokeless electronic cigarette."

"Yeah? The kind you plug in the wall?"

"No, it's a portable model," I said. "Runs on batteries—they're deceased."

He turned the object over in his fingers, sighted the barrel, smelled it. "Tell me, Rentadick, what's the point of smoking, if there's' no smoke? In fact, if there's no smoke, technically speaking you aren't smoking, are you? You're just pretending to be smoking, putting on a show. Faking it. So what's the point? Out with it! I want the truth!"

I responded that under less stressful circumstances I might be able to formulate an unambiguous answer to his abstruse existential question, yet found it difficult to concentrate with my hands hovering in the air while virtual strangers so flagrantly violated my personal space.

He gave me a long, mean, penetrating look. Then, "Okay, unfreeze, Rentadick. You can relax."

I lowered my arms, exhaled, relaxed…

"Freeze!" bellowed the second largest suit.

I froze.

The largest suit punched the second largest suit in the arm. "Agent Bissell, it was not your turn!" He turned to me. "I said unfreeze, Rentadick! Relax! And don't make me tell you again."

I unfroze.

"Freeze!" commanded the smallest of the three large suits.

I froze.

"Agent Kirby, will you knock it off!" growled the largest suit. "Only I get to say 'freeze!'"

Rather than chance that this was simply a rhetorical utterance, I froze on command.

"Damn it, Rentadick! Will you please unfreeze!"

Unfreezing, I said, "Hey, what's with the gumshoe boogie? Who are you guys?"

"I am special agent Orville Oreck of the FBI," said the largest suit. He motioned to the second largest suit, "This is adjunct special agent, Bissell."

"And who's the other suit?" I wanted to know.

"Agent Kirby, our spare."

"So, agents Oreck, Bissell and Kirby," I said. "Would I be correct in assuming there's also a suit named agent Dyson?"

"Dyson?" sneered Bissell. "That bagless shit!"

"Hey," Kirby objected. "Dyson's an upright guy in my book."

"You're Hoover's boys then?" I said.

"And proud of it," growled agent Oreck. "J. Edgar was a great man. As you know, he stamped out communism."

"Yes," I said, "a rather difficult feat in high heels, I would imagine."

"Watch it, Rentadick!" barked agent Oreck. "We're not here to discuss Mr. Hoover's idiosyncratic sartorial propensities."

I had to chuckle. "Although I am more than delighted to make your acquaintance, gentlemen," I said, "you must understand that I am not Mr. Rentadick."

"Then just where is Rentadick?" inquired agent Oreck.

"There is no Mr. Rentadick," I said.

"I don't understand," said agent Bissell.

I suspected that agent Kirby, too, was confused. "I'm confused," he said, as if to confirm my hunch.

"Look, gentlemen," I explained, "just because there's a name on the door doesn't mean there is a physical person of that name on the premises."

"But the Supreme Court—"

"Yes, yes, but look, I'm sorry—" I began.

"When's the last time you cleaned your carpets, Rentadick?" demanded agent Kirby.

"So that's it?" I nearly dissolved into laughter. "Okay, I get it—Oreck, Bissell, Kirby, Hoover. You guys are here to vacuum my carpets? Well, too late, I'm afraid. We just shampooed—"

Bissell jammed the barrel of his pistol hurtfully into my ribs, "Don't be a wise-ass, Rentadick. Just answer the question."

CHAPTER 10

I hit the intercom button. "Susie, when was the last time we cleaned the carpets?"

"Whom should I say is calling, please?"

"Dammit, Susie, it's me, your boss!"

"Oh...well, I don't remember no last time, boss."

"Come now, Susie, we just had the carpets shampooed sometime last month...what day was that?"

I turned to agent Oreck. "I don't understand. What do my carpets have to do with anything?"

"It's not so much your carpets as what's under them we're interested in."

Under the carpets? I cast him a glance of incredulity and again hit the intercom button. "Susie, have we ever, to your knowledge, swept anything under the carpet?"

"I tried once, boss. But they're all sort of glued down wall-to-wall, you know."

"So, gentlemen," I said, "there you have it."

Agent Oreck snarled, "Sit down, Rentadick!"

I looked around. "I *am* sitting," I said.

"Then stand up and sit down again!" He howled. "Who the hell is in charge here, anyway?"

I stood up and sat down again, per his ungracious request.

Agent Oreck came close to loom ominously over me. "So, tell me, Rentadick, what's under the carpet?"

"You heard Susie," I carefully explained. "How on earth can one sweep anything under a glued-down wall-to-wall carpet?"

"He's got a point, boss," said Agent Kirby.

Oreck rounded on him. "It was just a figure of speech, doofus; an analogy or metaphor or something like that."

"It's neither an analogy nor a metaphor," I spoke up. "It's an idiom; more precisely an idiomatic phrase."

Oreck raised his gun butt as if to hammer my head. "Who you calling an idiot, maggot?"

"Sorry, I was merely pointing out a grammatical error."

"Yeah, and who died and made you the grammar expert?"

"I happen to be an English Major." I said.

"Hey, fellas," crowed agent Bissell. "We got us a Major here." He turned to me, "Army?"

"A buck says he's Air Force," offered agent Kirby.

"Neither," I said. "I majored in the English language at Bryn Mawr."

Agent Bissell regarded me with curled eyebrow. "That's a girly college, ain't it?"

I shrugged. "Hey, what can I say? There were certain perks—"

Agent Kirby's mouth fell open. "You went to college to learn how to speak your own language?"

"To speak it well, yes."

"Are you perchance insinuating agents Oreck, Bissell and I don't speak good English?"

"Well enough to get by on a primal level," I said. "But in any sophisticated milieu—"

"Shut up!"said Oreck.

I acknowledged his succinct request by closing my mouth.

He then jammed his face close to mine so that I could easily ascertain that he had eaten something garlicky for lunch—on second thought, it must have been breakfast, since it was not yet lunchtime.

"Is it safe, Rentadick?" he said.

CHAPTER 11

I looked into agent Oreck's gleaming, narrowed eyes. "Safe?" I responded. "Is what safe?"

"Is it safe?"

"Is what safe?"

"Is it safe!" Agent Oreck bellowed.

"I'm awfully sorry," I explained, "I have no idea what you're yammering on about."

"Look Rentadick," said adjunct agent Bissell, "we heard you giving the dame directions to your broom closet. Mind telling us what's in the broom closet?"

I shrugged. "I don't know…brooms, mops, pails, that sort of thing, I suppose."

Grinning with evil intent, agent Oreck turned to Bissell and Kirby. "Looks like we got us a comedian here, boys. Agent Kirby, did you bring the water board?"

Agent Kirby grimaced and hung his head. "Sorry, boss, I forgot." He brightened. "But I got the nail extractors. Let's give him a Mafia manicure."

"I remembered the dental drill," piped agent Bissell.

"Good…" Agent Oreck turned to me once more, baring his teeth in a malicious smile. "Now, Rentadick…is it safe?"

"I don't have a safe," I said. "Do you see a safe anywhere around here?"

"Is it safe?"

"I don't have a safe!"

"Once more, is it safe?"

"I don't what you are talking about?"

"One last time, is it safe?"

"You want to keep your teeth and fingernails, pretty boy, you'll come clean," said agent Kirby.

"Come clean?" I said.

"Spill the beans," explained agent Bissell

"Spill the beans?"

"Sing like a little birdie," said agent Oreck.

"Look, fellows," I said, "this is so terribly redundant. It's beginning to wreak havoc on what's left of my nerves."

Oreck's eyes narrowed, he grinned wickedly. "So, Rentadick, you don't like redundancy, huh?"

"It drives me crazy," I confessed. "Makes me want to pull my hair out by the roots. The only thing worse is dangling participles."

"Hey, boss," said Kirby, "how about I dangle some participles?"

"No, please!" I cried. "Would you dare be so beastly cruel? If you have a shred of human decency—"

Oreck grinned maniacally. "Okay, Kirby, hit 'em!"

"Walking down Main Street, the trees were beautiful," taunted Kirby.

I squirmed. "Oh, God, *nooo…*!"

Oreck turned, "Now you, agent Bissell, chime in with some redundancy."

"Redundant! Redundant! Redundant!" Bissell crooned.

"Aarghh!" I cried out again and again. Oh, the inhumanity!

They came at me, unrelentingly, from right and left:

"Reaching the station, the sun came out."

"Redundant! Redundant! Redundant!"

On and on it went until my mind at last sailed into limbo. I lost all track of time. No man, however brave and strong, could survive such a sustained barrage of redundancy and dangling participles. I felt my head would explode. I just couldn't take any more. I was a broken man.

With what I thought was my last breath, I croaked, "Okay, stop! I'll talk, I'll spill anything. You want beans, you got beans, whatever. What kind of beans you want, pinto, lima, Boston-baked, what?"

"Okay boys," smiled agent Oreck, "I think our little canary is ready to sing."

"Sing? Sing about what?" I groaned.

"How about a few bars of The Givenchy Code?"

"Could you hum…?"

"Wise-ass!" Oreck was furious. "Kirby, hit Mr. wise guy here with another dangling participle."

"I saw the trailer, peeking through the window!"

"No! No! Please!" I howled in agony.

Then, mercifully, I passed out.

CHAPTER 12

When I came to, agents Oreck, Bissell and Kirby were slouched listlessly around my desk; Oreck sucking on my smokeless electronic cigarette, Bissell nonchalantly cleaning his nails, and Kirby, from the sound of it, evidently practicing his mantra yoga.

I looked at them; they looked at me.

"So, guys," I said, "what's the agenda?"

"Why don't you tell us, Rentadick," grumbled Oreck.

I thought for a minute. "Well," I said, "I suppose we could do something at this point to advance the story plotline."

"Like what, for instance?"

"I don't know," I said. "I'll have to give it some thought…"

"*Jesus Christ on a bike!*" howled Oreck. "Don't tell me we're gonna end up three characters in search of a plot again!"

"We can't just stand around doing nothing!" cried Bissell. "Look, Pecksniff, you're the protagonist here. It's up to you—"

"Well, I suppose we could do the scene over…"

"No way, Jose!"

"Okay, okay," I said. "Let's not panic. Tell you what, why don't you guys take a break. Go hide in the closet, and when I think of something I'll give you a shout. But Miss Pantzaroff is due here any minute, so hurry."

"Okay, okay," groused Oreck.

The three agents rose and headed reluctantly for the closet. Kirby shook his head, "Geez, I swear—you just can't make this stuff up!"

CHAPTER 13

Secretarial Susie and I were confabulating in the front office when the plaintive siren song of a saxophone reverberated the hallways—alert! A *femme fatale* on the premises! In a while, the door to the broom closet next door opened, closed, and shortly thereafter our office door creaked slowly open.

Miss Polinovska Pantzaroff entered the room in all her sensuous splendor, encased in a clinging, black sequined dress that faithfully revealed the outrageous curvilinear contours of her body. She was a geometrician's wet dream: a riotous symphony of undulating convex and concave polytopes arranged in complex parabolic configurations. Her divine Cartesian coordinates $(a+b/a=a/b)$ were indecently superb.

My immediate glandular response? *"Hooboy!"*

Miss Pantzaroff was, in a word, pulchritude incarnate. Her moist, succulent lips were like luscious, overly ripe bing cherries; her eyes—one green, one blue—smoldering embers veiled by incredibly long lashes feathering high Mongolian cheekbones.

While I engaged in evaluating Miss Pantzaroff's cardinal statistics, secretarial Susie made her own observations. She surveyed Miss Pantzaroff slowly up and down, rolled her eyes and lifted her nose dismissively. Miss Pantzaroff then glared at Susie under a superciliously curved eyebrow, and the room went electric with subliminal feline vibes. For a moment I caught a whiff of something that smelled suspiciously like burning cat fur and, for some odd reason, H. L. Mencken's definition of a misogynist sprang to mind. A misogynist, opined Mencken, is "a man who hates women as much as women hate one another."

I thought it best to quickly assert my manly prerogative, lest the situation carom out of hand.

"Ahem…Miss Pantzaroff…" I crooked my finger and beckoned judiciously, "would you step into my office, please?"

"Said the spider to the fly," quipped Susie.

"Please, this way, Miss Pantzaroff…" I urged.

Miss Pantzaroff paused. "But I vaunt to know vhat is about spider and fly."

"Please, Miss Pantzaroff, spiders and flies can wait—now please…"

Taking her firmly by one ravishing elbow, I guided her gently but masterfully to the entrance of my inner sanctum, held the door as she ankled into the room.

"How on earth do you do that?" I marveled.

"How do I do vhat?" She responded, wide-eyed.

"Walk on your ankles like that?"

"Oy, I vaunted so badly to be famous ballerina," she explained sheepishly. "But ankles they are veak. I bend them too much and they stay that way, I think."

My nose twitched; my toes curled, as the exotic fragrance of her undoubtedly ridiculously expensive perfume set my nostrils aquiver.

"Well, please have a seat," I said.

Miss Pantzaroff glanced about the room, somewhat bewildered, and wrinkled her alabaster brow. "But where is chairs? I do not see chair."

"Yes. Well, I'm afraid our furniture budget is somewhat restricted," I said. "You see, headquarters—"

"Ya, ya, I am know about headquarters. But where you vaunt me to sit, on floor?"

I made a gracious sweeping gesture. "Please take my chair there behind the desk," I said.

"But where then you will sit? On floor?"

"No, no," I said. "I'll stand."

"Nyet! I cannot sit and you stand."

I offered what I thought a perfectly logical solution. "How about we both stand?"

"But if both stand, then chair does not serve function as chair."

"I acknowledge your utilitarian ethos," I said. "But logical positivist that I am, it seems clear that we have but one chair and two people."

"Then maybe it means I am to sit on lap."

"Lap? Whose lap?" My Adams Apple quivered. I gulped. "Mine?"

She beamed; her eyes lit lasciviously, the lewd invitation of a smile played her lush lips, "You do not vaunt Miss Pantzaroff to sit on lap?"

CHAPTER 14

With Miss Pantzaroff comfortably planted in my lap it was time to get down to business.

"Now about this Givenchy Code—" I began, but then was given to pause. I said, sternly, "Must you?"

"Must I vhat?"

"Must you wriggle about in such a brazen manner?"

She regarded me, crestfallen, her eyes brimming with childish innocence. "You do not vaunt I to be moving on lap?"

"Moving is one thing," I said, "lap dancing altogether another."

"Vhat you mean I am dance on lap?"

"I mean your derriere appears to be doing…well, let's just say you've obviously had Rumba lessons."

"And vhat is derriere?"

"It's-it's French for, ah…let's see—bottom."

"Bottom?"

"You know" I said, "—rump, backside, bum, duff, fanny, rear, tush, buttocks…"

"Ya, and you do not vaunt tush to dance?"

"Not while I'm conducting business" I said. "I find it rather…well, hard to concentrate."

She grinned and proclaimed with guileless pride. "Ya, is hard, okay…"

"Please, must we indulge in double entendres?"

"And vhat is doubles—?"

"Oh, never mind," I said. "The fact, you see, is that I find you irresistibly attractive."

"Ya, is hard, okay…"

"Will you please stifle yourself!" I reprimanded. "In the interest of full disclosure, Miss Pantzaroff, I must inform you that I wish you to be the mother of my children."

She gazed at me in amazement. "How many children you have?"

"To be perfectly honest," I said, "actually none—none that I know of, at least."

"Then how is it I can be mother of children?"

"Let me rephrase that…" I cleared my throat. "I mean I would like to give you children."

"But vhat children do you vaunt to give me? You know somebody who is have children to give?"

"Well, no. But you see… Look here, what I mean is I would like to, ah…"

She brightened. "Oy! You like for me to give children!"

"Yes," I said, "I think that is the gist of what I'm trying—"

"But I am sorry that I have no children."

"Well…actually, I had *my* children in mind," I explained.

She made a confused, pouty face. "But you say you do not have children..."

"Look," I said, "we seem to be going around in circles, needlessly complicating the issue. Precisely what I had in mind is that I would like to help you make babies. If we make babies, then you can be the mother of my children, don't you see." I hastened to add, "Of course, they would be your children also. We would have joint custody, so to speak."

"And how you vaunt to help me make baby?"

"Well, we could start with a candlelit dinner at a nice Italian restaurant, and then repair to my place where I could put some romantic music on the stereo, and then we could slip into the boudoir—"

"Nyet!"

"Nyet what?" I said, taken aback. "What do you mean, Nyet?"

"I do not yet vaunt to be so animate."

"I really do think you mean 'intimate'," I said.

"Ya, animate is right word; I look it up."

"But animate means to move," I explained.

"Ya, is correct."

"Are you saying you don't want to move?"

"Ya...Nyet..."

"Not even when making love.?"

"How is people to move when make love?"

"Well...you...er, we, that is, we...I...and then you. It's somewhat difficult to explain without visuals," I said. "But I could give you a quick demonstration, if you like."

"Nyet. I do not vaunt now to demonstrate. Maybe demonstrate when we have solved Givenchy code."

"Then by all means," I said, "let's get cracking!"

CHAPTER 15

With ample motivation to lustily pursue the enigma of The Givenchy Code, I adjusted Miss Pantzaroff in my lap. "So, Miss Pantzaroff, fill me in on what you know about The Givenchy Code," I said. "I presume you refer to Hubert Givenchy, the famous French fashion designer."

"Nyet. Is about his many times great grandfather, Leonardo Givenchy."

"Leonardo Givenchy?" I said. "Why does that name sound so oddly familiar?"

"Ya, in old times he is pretty big in making clothes business. Most famous, he make vhat men to wear between legs."

"My goodness, he invented the codpiece?"

"Ya, I do think so. He also make other many things not to mention."

"Unmentionables, you mean?" I said. "Old Leonardo seems to have been a sort of the medieval Victoria Secrets. But still I don't understand—"

"Is about clothes fashion."

"I'm afraid I don't know much about fashion," I admitted.

"Ya, that I can see from awful suit."

"Never mind my awful suit," I said. "Tell me, where does the crazed albino with the meat cleaver fit into all this?"

"He belongs to ancient order of Knights Template."

"Knights Template, huh? What's that, some sort of esoteric cult?"

"Ya, is secret order vhat swears to protect fashion of Leonardo Givenchy."

"I see, the protectors of Leonardo's fashion design templates. But why exactly is this crazed albino after you, Miss Pantzaroff?"

"Because before he kill my father, he tell me big secret."

"The albino told you a big secret?" I said, seeking clarification.

"Nyet. *Father* is tell big secret before albino kill *him*."

"So your father told the albino a big secret?"

"Nyet! Father is tell *me* big secret!"

"I see," I said. "And what sort of big secret are we talking about here?"

Her multi-hued eyes widened, fearful. "Big secret that is to explode world."

"Might you be a little more specific?"

Miss Pantzaroff looked around and lowered her voice to a whisper. "Ya. Before he die, my father discovers secret code sewn in labels of Leonardo Givenchy's clothes. When code deciphered, it will reveal to the world ancient Vatican plot to hide truth."

"So you think the Vatican is behind this?"

"Ya, and real truth…"

"Real truth?" I said. "The real truth about what?"

She looked at me. Her eyes narrowed. "I think you cannot maybe handle real truth…"

"Hey, don't pull a Jack Nicholson on me!" I said.

She paused for a long moment in seeming trepidation before responding, "Okay. Real truth is that Mary Magdalene in bible is not woman."

"Mary Magdalene not a woman?" I recoiled in disbelief. "If Mary Magdalene was not a woman, then what was she?"

"She was man."

"Now wait. Wait just a minute!" I said. "Mary Magdalene was a man? Are you quite sure?"

"Ya, for sure, Mary Magdalene was not woman."

"But Mary is a woman's name…"

"Ya. But Mary is not real name. Real name is Murray."

I caught my breath. "*Murray* Magdalene? You can't be serious."

She drew back, wide-eyed. "Oy, vhat you think—maybe somebody can make this up?"

CHAPTER 16

I shifted the voluptuous, squirming Miss Pantzaroff on my lap. "In summary then, you're telling me that in DaVinci's painting of the Last Supper, the guy next to Jesus whom looks suspiciously like a woman, and whom some conjecture to be Mary Magdalene, was actually a guy named Murray?"

"Ya, for sure is Murray Magdalene."

"Then who, may I ask, was Mary Magdalene?"

"Murray is have sister."

I stroked my cheeks and tweaked my nose, as was my habit when on the verge of significant discovery. "Murray and Mary, the Magdalene siblings...umm, that explains a lot."

"Vhat does explain?"

"I'm not exactly sure at the moment," I said, "but it's bound to have significant bearing on the case. Now what else can you tell me about *Mary* Magdalene?"

"Oy, she is not so pretty like Murray."

"You're telling me she was ugly?"

"Ya, she is ugly and people on street throw stones."

"Let me get this straight," I said. "You're saying Mary Magdalene was so god-awful ugly that people threw stones at her?"

"Ya, and this is how she meet Jesus."

"Jesus threw stones at her?" I gasped. "Wow, that's some fearsome ugly, all right!"

It was beginning to dawn on me how such an explosive revelation would rock the very foundations of Christianity, not to mention the fashion industry. But I needed more clarification.

"Tell me, Miss Pantzaroff," I said, "Why was Murray Magdalene present at the Last Supper?"

"Because Murray is vhat in Russia we call first-class sponge."

"You mean a mooch?" I said. "A free loader?"

"Ya. If there is free meal, Murray is there with balls on."

"I do think you mean 'bells'," I said. "But let's not quibble—why do you suppose in those days people sat on only one side of the table during meals?"

"Oy, at Last Supper they vaunt to pose for picture, don't you think? If everybody sit all around table, we see back of somebody's head."

"That makes good sense," I said. "So you think Jesus and the Apostles posed for the picture?"

"Ya, is vhat today we call photo op."

The intercom buzzed in its usual obnoxious fashion.
I punched a button. "Yes..?"

"It's Susie, boss."

"No kidding…"

"Yes, really, boss."

"So…?"

"You have a visitor, boss."

"And who is it?" I said.

"This really weird looking guy…"

"Like how really weird looking?"

"Well, he's big and bald and sort of hunchback, and has tattoos all over…and he's drooling on his shoes—"

"Is he by any chance swinging a meat cleaver?" I wanted to know.

"It looks like one, boss, but let me ask…He says 'no'."

"No?"

"Yes…I mean, he said no. He says it's an ax."

"An *ax*!" I exclaimed. "Well, tell him he's dead wrong—tell him he doesn't know an ax from a hole in the ground. What he's slinging about is decidedly a cleaver."

"My goodness, boss," breathed Susie, "what's the difference?"

"We haven't time to go into such subtle semantics just now, Suzie," I explained. "But would you say the gentleman is deficient in pigmentation?"

"I guess. He's really pale looking and has shiny pink eyes."

"Yep," I said, "sounds like our crazed albino, all right."

A note of alarm crept into Susie's voice. "Crazed albino! What crazed albino, boss?"

"Oh, never mind, Susie," I said. "Tell him we don't take walk-ins. What does he think this is, a unisex salon?"

"…He says he don't care, boss; that he don't have no hair anyway."

I sighed. "Please admonish the gentleman not to use double negatives in my office, would you, Susie," I said. "Tell him, don't make come out there—and what is he doing now?"

"He's just standing here drooling and clutching that awful cleaver ax thing, flagellating himself, and mumbling Rentadick-Rentadick-Rentadick over and over."

"How horribly redundant!" I exclaimed. "But for God's sake, Susie, tell him there is no Mr. Rentadick. Explain the Supreme Court's decision was a mistake, that companies are not really people."

"I'm kinda afraid to make him mad, boss…"

"Well, he's already mad as a hatter, isn't he? So just tell him I'm busy," I said, "and to wait in the broom closet."

"In the broom closet, boss?"

"Yes, explain to him it's our temporary waiting room while we update the décor. Make him comfortable, why don't you? Give him a magazine with lots of pictures to read."

"Okay, if you say so, boss…"

"And by the way, Susie," I said, "Miss Pantzaroff and I will be ducking down the back fire escape for bit of lunch. Would you care for anything?"

"How about a Starbuck's mocha supreme latte."

"You got it, kid."

"And, boss…"

"Yeah, Susie?"

"Boss…it's getting real crazy weird around here. Tell me straight, wouldja—ain't nobody can make this stuff up, right?"

(to be continued…or not)